The Little Shot Series, Book One

The Little Shot
Courage

D1410680

By Tasha Eizinger
Illustrated by Miranda Meeks

GROUND TRUTH PRESS
NASHUA, NEW HAMPSHIRE

The Little Shot Series, Book One

Published by

GROUND TRUTH PRESS
P. O. Box 7313
Nashua, NH 03060-7313

Illustrations and Cover Design: Miranda Meeks

Editor: Bonnie Lyn Smith

Technical Editor: Melissa Hicks

PowerV® is a trademark owned by, and use of the PowerV® words is under a license from, MetaMetrics, Inc. All rights reserved.

Trade paperback ISBN-13: 978-1-7337677-8-1
Trade paperback ISBN-10: 1-7337677-8-9
Second printing edition, 2020
Printed in the United States of America

Second Edition
10 9 8 7 6 5 4 3 2

Publisher's Cataloging-In-Publication Data
(Prepared by The Donohue Group, Inc.)

Names: Eizinger, Tasha, author. I Meeks, Miranda, illustrator.
Title: The Little Shot. Courage / by Tasha Eizinger ; illustrated by Miranda Meeks.
Other Titles: Courage
Description: Second edition. I Nashua, New Hampshire : Ground Truth Press, [2020] I Series: The Little Shot series ; book 1 I Includes keyword index. I Interest age level: 008-012. I Summary: "Little Shot is a star with a nearly impossible dream! She wants to become a Big Shot, a shooting star, to give hope to the people below. Initially, she experiences both ridicule by her peers who don't share her vision, and setbacks when she seemingly fails at first. However, with her mentor's guidance and a courageous spirit, she perseveres until she achieves her big dream"--Provided by publisher.
Identifiers: ISBN 9781733767781 (trade paperback) I ISBN 1733767789 (trade paperback) I ISBN 9781733767798 (ebook)
Subjects: LCSH: Stars--Juvenile fiction. I Courage--Juvenile fiction. I Meteors--Juvenile fiction. I Self-actualization (Psychology)--Juvenile fiction. I CYAC: Stars--Fiction. I Courage--Fiction. I Meteors--Fiction. I Self-actualization (Psychology)--Fiction.
Classification: LCC PZ7.1.E59 Li 2020 (print) I LCC PZ7.1.E59 (ebook) I DDC [Fic]--dc23

Library of Congress Control Number: 2020901228

This book is dedicated to my sweet Little Shot and to *all* the Little Shots.

★★★★★

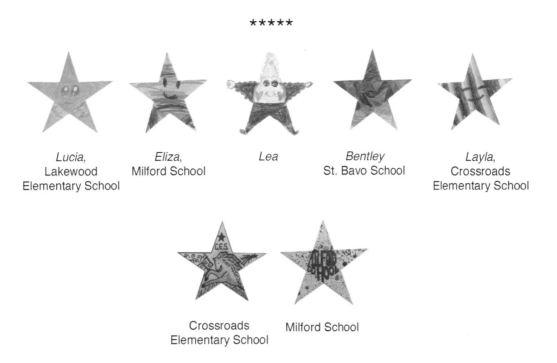

Lucia,
Lakewood
Elementary School

Eliza,
Milford School

Lea

Bentley
St. Bavo School

Layla,
Crossroads
Elementary School

Crossroads
Elementary School

Milford School

Thank you to the Little Shots who decorated a star featured in this book!

★★★★★

Thank you to everyone who has contributed to *The Little Shot*, with special mention of:

"A big shot is a little shot that kept shooting."

Originally a quote of American journalist and essayist Christopher Morley (1890-1957),
I first heard it referenced in Zig Ziglar's *See You at the Top* (Pelican Publishing, 1982).

My mentor, Chris Estes, for referencing this quote and being a living example of it

Our family, friends, and loving critics who pushed our book to the next level

Beta Viewers: Crysta Bowyer, Rebecca Tarman, Curtis Valentine, Nate and Susan Wessels

Beta Readers: Stacy Brantley, Christine Carter, Elisa Cothron, Pollyanne Kimmel, Tina Martin

Our very accommodating digital assistant Jannette Parent

Little Shot was mesmerized as she watched the Big Shots
and wondered if she could ever become a shooting star.

She decided to seek counsel from her family.

"Mom, do you think I could become a Big Shot? I would love to give people hope!"

Her mom lovingly said, "Little Shot, I believe in you! After all, 'a Big Shot is a Little Shot that kept shooting.'"

6

"Dad, how do I become a Big Shot?"

"You must make sacrifices."

7

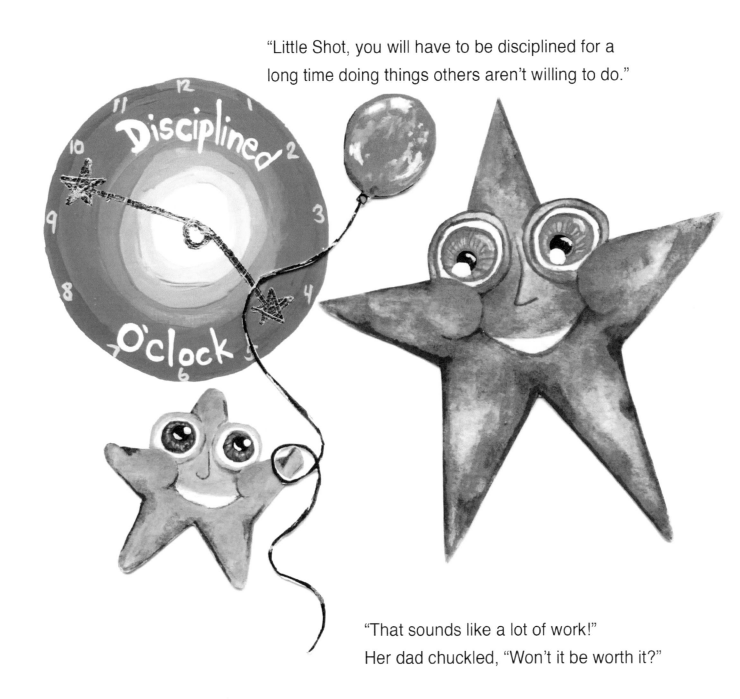

"Little Shot, you will have to be disciplined for a long time doing things others aren't willing to do."

"That sounds like a lot of work!"
Her dad chuckled, "Won't it be worth it?"

8

The twinkle came back to Little Shot's eyes.
"Yes! I could give people hope!"

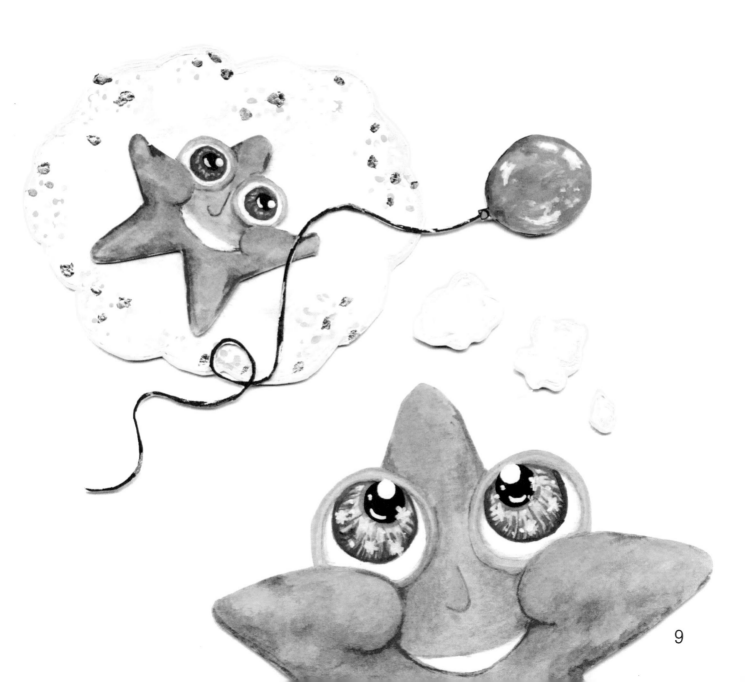

"Grandma, I want to be a Big Shot."

Her wise grandma answered solemnly, "I also wanted to be a Big Shot."

"You did?" responded stunned Little Shot.

"Yes, but I didn't have courage."

"What's courage?" asked Little Shot.

"Courage is leading from your heart despite your fear.
I now realize my greatest regrets are not the times
I tried and failed but rather the times I lacked
the courage to try. I also should have asked a Big Shot for mentorship."

Some of Little Shot's classmates had goals for their lives, and others did not. She was the only one who wanted to become a shooting star.

Two of her classmates made fun of her.

"Don't waste your time!"
"There's no way you can do it!"

Discouraged, Little Shot quietly said, "Maybe I don't want to be a Big Shot after all."

Little Shot needed a friend.

One dear friend said, "You are hardworking. If you learn the steps, you can make it happen."

I believe in YOU!

Clinging to those encouraging words, she mustered up the courage to speak with the Big Shots.

The Big Shots were warming up for another night of hope-filled fun.

Little Shot bashfully asked, "Can you mentor me?"

One Big Shot beamed, "Absolutely! We love paying forward the kindness of others!"

"Paying forward?"

"Someone showed us the way, so we simply ask that you help another Little Shot someday."

17

Little Shot was thankful and ready to learn.

It was hard work!

After consistent practice, she was ready for her big night.

She could hardly contain her excitement and her nervousness!

3... 2... 1...

20

WISHOOO

"Oh, no!" Little Shot shouted desperately.
She was falling, not shooting!

She felt her mentor's hand reach down to lift her.

"I am a failure and have wasted your time," Little Shot whispered.

"Chin up, Little Shot! This is how you learn.
Failure is an event, not your identity!
What do you think you did well?"

Amazed, Little Shot responded, "I'm really glad I did it despite my fear."

"YES! What is one thing you could do better?"

"Just one?"

"Yes, Little Shot, only one."

"To shoot longer, I need to be stronger."

"Great! Remember every attempt is a learning opportunity, and each attempt will make you stronger."

Little Shot kept practicing.

Some nights she progressed.

Some nights she regressed.

The fire in her heart kept her going until she was ready to soar.

3... 2... 1...

WISHHHH

Finally, she was a Big Shot, and it felt exhilarating!

She looked down knowing somebody was looking up at her while making a wish upon a shooting star.

30

Courage

My Big Shot Journal

1.) Believe in myself.
2.) Work hard and make sacrifices for a long time.
3.) Seek advice from a trustworthy adult.
4.) Have courage.
5.) Ask a Big Shot for mentorship.

Hope

Pay it Forward

Discipline

Failure... Learning Opportunity

Sacrifices

Little Shot is a star with a nearly impossible dream! She wants to become a Big Shot, a shooting star, to give hope to the people below. Initially, she experiences both ridicule by her peers, who don't share her vision, and setbacks when she seemingly fails. However, with her mentor's guidance and a courageous spirit, she perseveres until she improves and achieves her big dream.

Little Shot teamed up with The Lexile® PowerV® Vocabulary API & Service to offer this enriching vocabulary list. Dive right in and see how many Lexile PowerV words you can find in this book. Read along with a partner and tell them what each word means.

Consistent	**Mentor**	**Trustworthy**
Counsel	**Mentorship**	**Twinkle**
Courage	**Reach**	**Vision**
Dive	**Ridicule**	**Waste**
Event	**Seek**	**Wise**
Identity	**Soar**	**Worth**
Improve	**Spirit**	

CPSIA information can be obtained
at www.ICGtesting.com
Printed in the USA
BVRC090734240921
617231BV00003B/1

Author Tasha Eizinger has a big heart for writing books that provide inspiration and a path for children to live out their dreams. Much of this passion has stemmed from how she was raised—dream big, and go for it! As a former elementary school teacher, she has enjoyed reconnecting with children and teachers through The Little Shot series while speaking in schools. Tasha, her husband, and their own Big-Shot-in-the-making live in northern Indiana. Tasha loves swimming, reading, cooking, traveling, and meeting other dreamers!

Illustrator Miranda Meeks strongly believes that art is not meant to be perfect—it's meant to be made—stories should be told, and every Little Shot has a story worth telling. As a former collegiate distance runner, she understands the importance of pace, hard work, determination, and belief in one's self when it comes to chasing big dreams. Miranda is an art teacher in her native Kentucky where she loves who and what she teaches.

LEXILE®

Lexile® measure:
480L

@littleshotseries

www.thelittleshot.com

fb.com/thelittleshot

ISBN 9781733767781

9 781733 767781

T3-ABI-265